For Chloe, Lucy, Zach and Nate

G. P. PUTNAM'S SONS

A division of Penguin Young Readers Group

Published by The Penguin Group

Penguin Group (USA) Inc., 345 Hudson Street, New York, NY 10014, U.S.A.

Penguin Group (Canada), 10 Alcorn Avenue, Toronto, Ontario, Canada M4V 3B2 (a division of Pearson Penguin Canada Inc.)

Penguin Books Ltd, 80 Strand, London WC2R 0RL, England.

Penguin Ireland, 25 St. Stephen's Green, Dublin 2, Ireland (a division of Penguin Books Ltd.)

Penguin Group (Australia), 250 Camberwell Road, Camberwell, Victoria 3124, Australia (a division of Pearson Australia Group Pty Ltd).

Penguin Books India Pvt Ltd, 11 Community Centre, Panchsheel Park, New Delhi - 110 017, India.

Penguin Group (NZ), Cnr Airborne and Rosedale Roads, Albany, Auckland 1310, New Zealand (a division of Pearson New Zealand Ltd).

Penguin Books (South Africa) (Pty) Ltd, 24 Sturdee Avenue, Rosebank, Johannesburg 2196, South Africa.

Penguin Books Ltd, Registered Offices: 80 Strand, London WC2R 0RL, England.

Manufactured in China by South China Printing Co. Ltd.

Design by Gina DiMassi. Text set in Barbera Fat. The art was done with cut paper, charcoal and colored pencils.

Library of Congress Cataloging-in-Publication Data   Horowitz, Dave, 1970–

The ugly pumpkin / by Dave Horowitz.

p. cm.   Summary: A lonely, oddly-shaped pumpkin is sad that no one chose him for Halloween,

but by Thanksgiving he has discovered where he belongs.

[1. Pumpkins—Fiction. 2. Identity—Fiction. 3. Halloween—Fiction. 4. Thanksgiving Day—Fiction. 5. Stories in rhyme.]

I. Title.   PZ8.3.H784SUg 2005   [E]—dc22   2004016576   ISBN 0-399-24267-8

5 7 9 10 8 6

The UGLY PUMPKIN

by

dave horowitz

G. P. PUTNAM'S SONS

NEW YORK

I

am the ugly pumpkin,
as you can plainly see.
Of one hundred thousand pumpkins,
none are quite like me.

Since early in October
I've been waiting to get picked,
but each time things start looking up . . .

I end up
getting tricked.

A skeleton came for pumpkins
one bright and crispy day.

Going
MY WAY?

I asked if I could
get a ride . . .
He laughed and said:

NO WAY

And when I said,
"It's getting late,
and I don't have a home."
He rolled his eye,
said, "Good-bye,"

and left me
all alone.

So I walked into November,
where I happened on some trees.
I asked if I could stay awhile,
and this time I said:

The trees all
started smiling,
and then one
finally spoke:

"Take off yer boots
and spread yer roots . . ."

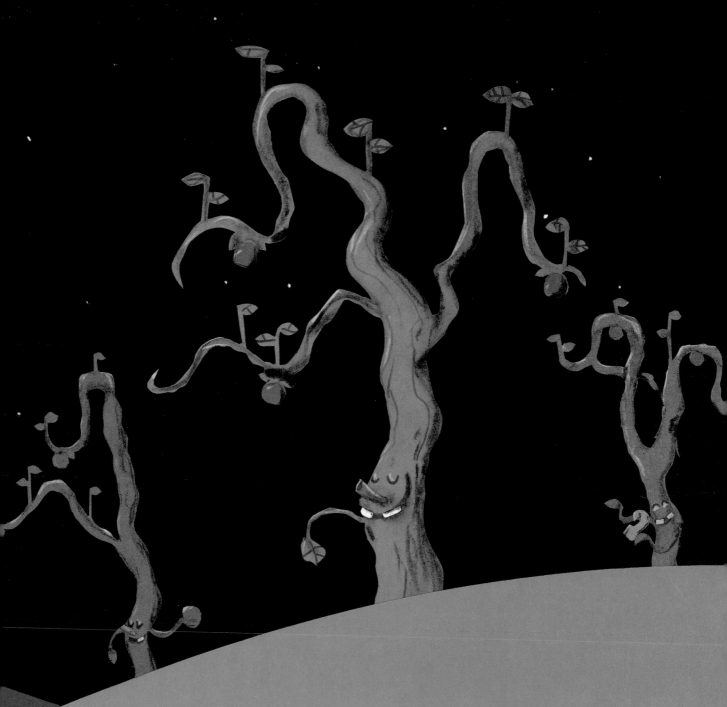

Another cruel joke.

I AM THE UGLY PUMPKIN!

I shouted to the sky.

And then it started raining,
so I began to cry.

I took shelter in a garden
that was overrun with squash.

I noticed something
very odd
and then thought,
O my gosh . . .

At last it was Thanksgiving
and I found where I fit in.
Now you know my story,
so let the feast begin.